Dedicated to my little girl, who teaches me new things every day.

I hope you enjoy playing with your little ones as much as I do with mine playing with this book.

Martina Molina

What does the duck say?

Quack Quack

what does the chick say?

peep peep

what does the sheep say?

baa baa

What does the cow say?

moo moo

what does the rooster say?

cock-a-doodle-doo

what does the chicken say?

cluck cluck

what does the horse say?

neigh neigh

what does the donkey say?

hee-haw hee-haw

what does the dog say?

what does the cat say?

meow meow

what does the rabbit say?

click click

what does the owl say?

hoo – h'hoo – hoo – hoo

What does the wolf say?

owooooo owooooo

How does the snake say?

hisss hisss

What does the frog say?

croak croak

What does the lion say?

roar roar

What does the elephant say?

toot toot

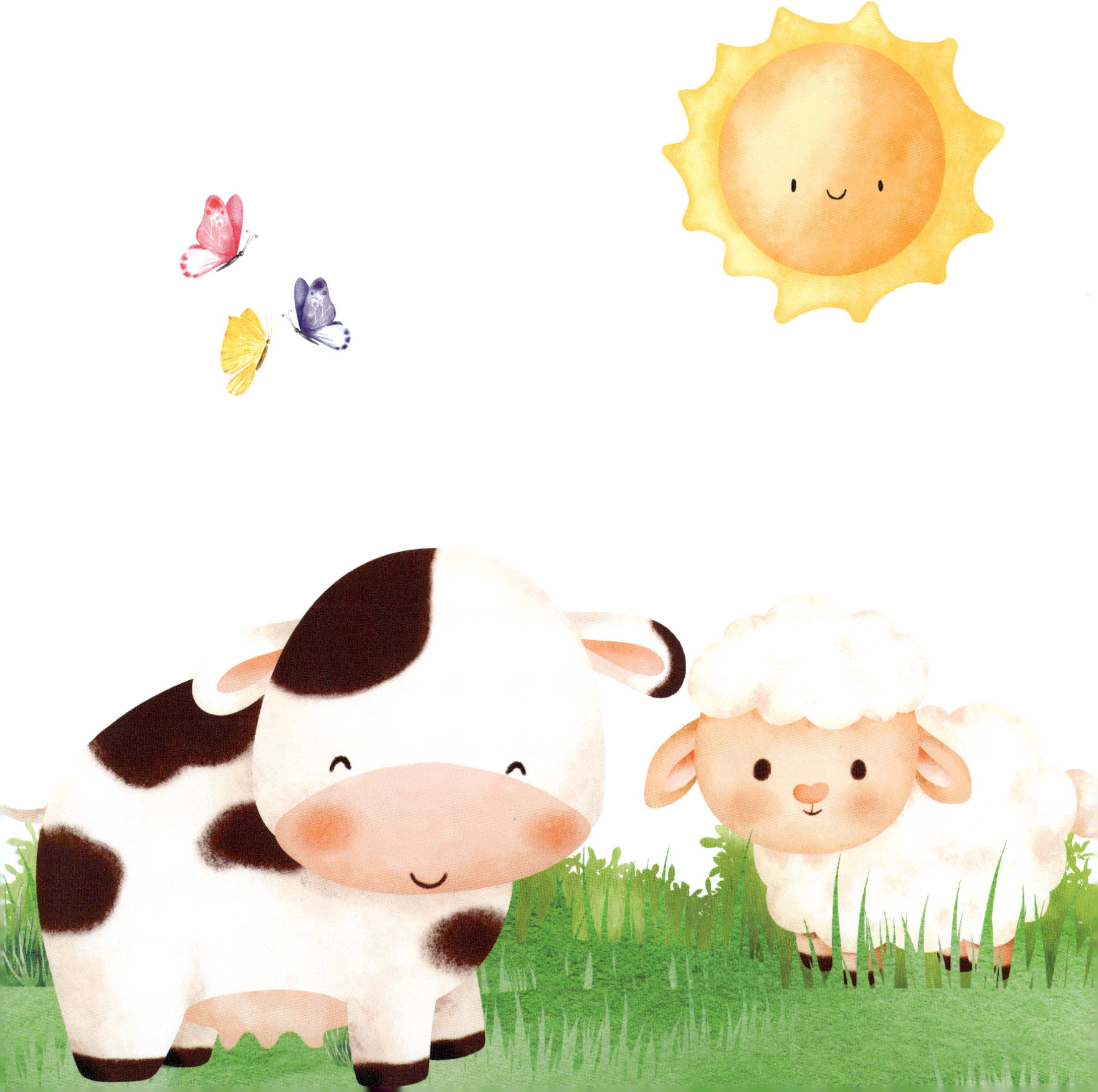

Printed in Great Britain
by Amazon